WUTHERING HEIGHTS

WUTHERING HEIGHTS

By Emily Brontë

Adapted by Betty Ren Wright
Illustrated by Helen Cogancherry

Raintree Publishers • Milwaukee • Toronto • Melbourne • London

Library of Congress Number: 81-15786

Printed and bound in the United States of America.

Library of Congress Cataloging in Publication Data

Wright, Betty Ren.
  Wuthering Heights.

  Summary: In nineteenth-century Yorkshire, the passionate attachment between a headstrong young girl and a foundling boy brought up by her father causes disaster for them and many others, even in the next generation.
  I. Brontë, Emily, 1818-1848.   Wuthering Heights.
II. Shaw, Charles, 1941-   ill.   III. Title.
PZ7.W933Wu [Fic]   81-15786
ISBN 0-8172-1682-0   AACR2

CONTENTS

CHAPTER ONE

1801

I have just returned from a visit to my landlord and only neighbor Mr. Heathcliff. It is a beautiful walk from my new residence Thrushcross Grange to his home, known as Wuthering Heights. We are far removed from society, here on the Yorkshire moors.

Heathcliff looks like a dark-skinned gypsy, handsome but reserved. Certainly he is not a man to show warmth easily. I was received into a large and cheerful room, but with little show of interest from its master. A sour-faced servant named Joseph brought wine, and my host and I discussed the countryside. When I suggested another visit, it was easy to see Mr. Heathcliff did not wish it. Still, I shall go, anyway. I feel quite sociable when I compare myself with him.

Yesterday I walked again over the moors to Wuthering Heights. I arrived just as it began to snow. Joseph shouted at me from the barn but did not offer to open the door of the house. At last a rough-looking young man appeared and led me inside.

A lovely young girl was there. Golden ringlets hung at her neck, and her eyes would have been beautiful, except that they were full of scorn. She pouted like a child about to cry.

The young man stared down on me, and I began to doubt that he was a servant. He looked shabby and bearish, but his manner was haughty. It was a relief when Mr. Heathcliff appeared.

"You should not ramble in a snow storm," he said. "You might easily be lost."

"Could you spare me a guide?" I asked.

"No, I could not. Get the tea ready," he said to the girl roughly.

I was directed to the table, where I learned through questions that the girl was Heathcliff's daughter-in-law. I assumed then that she was the wife of the rough boor who sat with us, but I was wrong.

"He is not my son," Heathcliff said. "My son is dead."

"My name is Hareton Earnshaw," growled the youth. "You'd better respect it!"

After tea, I discovered that outside all was a bitter whirl of wind and snow.

"Let this be a lesson to you to make no more rash journeys," Heathcliff said. "I have no room for visitors."

I was so disgusted that I rushed from the house and snatched up a lantern in the barn, resolving to walk home anyway. At once Joseph shouted "Thief!" and set the dogs after me. It was the housekeeper who drove them off; Heathcliff and Earnshaw only laughed.

Back in the house, the master offered me brandy and told the housekeeper, Zillah, to find me a bed. Since I felt quite faint, I was forced to accept the offer.

On the way upstairs Zillah told me not to make a noise, because the master had some odd notion about the room she would put me in. He never wanted anybody to sleep there. She did not know the reason.

The room had little furniture. The bed was enclosed like a small closet. It had a window, the ledge of which served as a table. Books were piled on this ledge, and I discovered they carried the names Catherine Earnshaw, Catherine Heathcliff, or Catherine Linton. Every inch of blank paper in these books was covered with writing — a kind of diary.

"An awful Sunday!" one page began. "I wish my father were back. My brother Hindley is so cruel to Heathcliff! He won't let him sit with us, nor eat with us. He blames our father for treating Heathcliff too well, and he swears he will reduce him to his right place."

As I read, I began to nod over the dim page. A terrible night followed. I dreamed I was lying in the bed, listening to a fir tree rattle against the windowpane. To stop it, I broke the pane and stretched an arm through the hole. At once, the fingers of an icy cold little hand closed on my arm.

"Let me in!" sobbed a voice. "I am Catherine Linton. I have wandered on the moor for twenty years."

I was maddened with fear. "How can I let you in?" I said. "Let me go first!"

The fingers relaxed, and I snatched my arm away. I piled books in front of the broken pane. Still the wailing continued, and then the books moved as if they were pushed. I shouted aloud in a frenzy of fright. A moment later I awoke as Heathcliff burst into my room.

His face was white. "Who put you here?" he cried.

"Your servant Zillah," I retorted. "And it is swarming with ghosts." I described to him my dream, while I hurriedly dressed. As I left the room, I looked back and saw him wrench open the window.

"Come in!" he cried. "Oh, my darling Catherine, hear me *this* time at last!" There was such anguish in his cry that I was sorry I had told my dream.

I hurried downstairs, and when dawn came I escaped to the icy outdoors. Heathcliff soon followed and offered to guide me home. It was well he did, or I would have been hopelessly lost. He left me at the gate of the Grange, and before long my housekeeper, Mrs. Dean, was welcoming me home. She had believed me dead in the storm!

I was numbed to the heart by my experience. Even now I am feeble as a kitten — almost too much so to enjoy my fire and my coffee.

I had planned to keep entirely to myself, but by dusk I found myself urging Mrs. Dean to sit and talk while I ate

dinner. I had many questions about Wuthering Heights.

Mrs. Dean was a willing gossip. I learned that Wuthering Heights had once belonged to the Earnshaws. Catherine and Hindley Earnshaw lived there with their parents, and Mrs. Dean, the child of a servant, had grown up there, too. One day Mr. Earnshaw returned from a business trip with a dirty, ragged, black-haired child. He had found the boy starving in the city.

Mrs. Earnshaw and the children would have nothing to do with him, but Mr. Earnshaw insisted that he stay. He named the child Heathcliff for a son who had died in childhood.

Hindley beat and pinched the newcomer whenever he could, and his father punished him for it. Heathcliff became the old man's favorite, for Catherine was too full of mischief to be a pet.

So, from the beginning Heathcliff caused bad feeling. Two years later Mrs. Earnshaw died, and Mr. Earnshaw began to grow feeble. Hindley went away to college, and Catherine and Heathcliff became closest friends.

Catherine was a wild, wicked girl, with a bonny eye and a sweet smile. She could make Heathcliff do anything she wished. Each day she teased and worried her father, made fun of Joseph, baited Mrs. Dean, and spent most of her time with Heathcliff.

Then one evening their little world came to an end. Catherine went to her father to kiss him good night and found him dead. Mrs. Dean joined in the tears of the two children.

Later that night the housekeeper went up to their room and found them consoling each other. No parson ever pictured heaven so beautifully as they did. While Mrs. Dean sobbed and listened, she could not help wishing they were all there safe together.

CHAPTER TWO

Hindley came home to his father's funeral and brought a wife with him, Mrs. Dean continued. The bride was a loving, lighthearted girl, and she became very fond of Catherine. She disliked Heathcliff, however, and that aroused all of Hindley's old hatred. Hindley told Heathcliff he must give up his lessons and work and live with the servants.

Heathcliff bore up pretty well at first, because he and Catherine were together whenever possible. Often they ran away to the moors and stayed all day, little caring for the beatings that awaited them at home.

One night, after the others had gone to bed, Heathcliff came home alone.

"Where is Miss Catherine?" cried Mrs. Dean.

He said she was at Thrushcross Grange. They had gone there to peek through a window and see how the Linton family passed their Sunday evenings. Someone loosed a bulldog on them, and it had seized Catherine by the ankle.

Heathcliff had tried with all his power to cram a stone down the beast's throat, but to no avail. At last a servant arrived, and Catherine was carried into the house. Heathcliff followed, swearing at them all.

The Lintons were shocked to see who it was their dog had caught. Catherine was made comfortable, while Edgar and Isabella, the two children, stared in fascination. The Lintons made such unpleasant comments about Heathcliff's gypsy looks that he swore at them again. Heathcliff

was pronounced " a wicked boy, quite unfit for a decent house," and was ordered away. He watched through a window while the family fussed over Catherine.

The next day Mr. Linton came to Wuthering Heights and gave Hindley a lecture on how to look after his family. Catherine stayed at the Grange to recover. Heathcliff was told that when she returned he was not to speak one word to her or he would be dismissed.

Catherine lived at Thrushcross Grange till Christmas. When she returned home, she was a dignified young lady with fine manners. She looked for Heathcliff at once, but when he came forward, all covered with grime, she kissed him and laughed.

"How black and cross you look!" she said. "But that's because I'm used to Edgar and Isabella Linton."

Heathcliff dashed off in a rage, amid the merriment of Hindley and his wife. Catherine was surprised. She didn't understand why he was angry.

The next day the Linton children were to come for a visit. Heathcliff cleaned himself up, but the day went badly. Edgar treated him with contempt, and Hindley ordered him to stay in the kitchen. That night Heathcliff swore he would some day get revenge on them both.

At this point Mrs. Dean broke off her story, fearing I was getting tired. When she saw I was truly interested, however, she agreed to go on.

"I will jump to the next summer," she said, "the summer of 1778."

In that year a baby boy was born to the Earnshaws. Soon afterward, Mrs. Earnshaw, always delicate, died, and Mrs. Dean was given little Hareton to raise.

Hindley Earnshaw neither wept nor prayed. He gave himself up to drink and bad living. Before long, the housekeeper and Joseph were the only servants willing to stay at the Heights.

Catherine continued her friendship with the Lintons. At

home she was with Heathcliff constantly, though at sixteen he was a grim, repulsive youth. He had forgotten his early schooling, and he worked long hours. He adored Catherine, but he no longer put his fondness in words. Catherine did little to soothe his jealousy of the Lintons.

"Why should I always be with you?" she would ask him. "You say and do nothing to amuse me!"

One day, when Edgar came calling, he saw Catherine at her worst. Hindley had told Mrs. Dean to remain in the room when his sister had a caller, and so she did, in spite of pinches and cruel words. Edgar was shocked at Catherine's behavior, but such was his attraction to her that he willingly forgave her when she began to cry.

Later that evening Catherine came to the kitchen. Mrs. Dean thought Heathcliff was in the barn and so let her talk freely. Only later did she realize he was there in the kitchen, sitting in the shadows while they spoke.

"Nelly, will you keep a secret?" Catherine began. "Edgar has asked me to marry him, and I've accepted him. He is handsome and pleasant and young, and he loves me."

"Do you love him?" the housekeeper asked.

"Of course," she said. "Yet in my soul and in my heart I believe I am wrong to marry him. I dreamt I was in heaven once, and I broke my heart wanting to come back to Earth. I wanted only to be here. If my brother had not brought Heathcliff so low, all would be different. But it would degrade me to marry Heathcliff now, so he shall never know how I love him. You see, he is more myself than I am, Nelly. Whatever our souls are made of, his and mine are the same. Linton's is as different as a moonbeam from lightning."

Mrs. Dean became aware of Heathcliff's presence then as he stole from the kitchen. He had heard Catherine say it would degrade her to marry him, and he had stayed no longer.

She rattled on, saying that after she was married she would still be Heathcliff's friend. Edgar would have to

learn to tolerate him. She would use Edgar's money, she said, to help Heathcliff escape her brother's power.

"I *am* Heathcliff," she said. "Our love is like the eternal rocks — a source of little visible delight, but necessary."

They talked on until a storm came up. When Mrs. Dean went looking for Heathcliff, he was nowhere to be found. She was forced to tell Catherine that he had heard part of their conversation, and the girl was wildly distressed. She ran about outside, calling and sobbing. Nor would she remove her wet things when she finally came in. She sat by the fire and was still there the next morning. It was soon clear that she was dangerously ill.

The doctor was called. Catherine lay sick a long time, and at last she was carried off to the Grange to be cared for. The Lintons suffered much for that kindness. Both Mr. and Mrs. Linton caught the fever and died within a few days of each other.

Heathcliff was not heard from again. Mrs. Dean told Catherine his going was her own fault, and the girl did not speak to the housekeeper for months. The doctor insisted that the invalid must have her own way or she would become sick again, so her fiery temper went unchecked. But Edgar still loved her and felt himself the happiest man alive when he led her to Gimmerton Chapel, three years after his parents' death.

Against Mrs. Dean's will she went with Catherine to live at the Grange. She did not want to leave little Hareton, but both Catherine and Hindley insisted, so she had to kiss the child good-bye.

At this point Mrs. Dean discovered the time was half-past one. She would not stay a minute longer. Now that I have thought about her story for another hour, I am ready for bed also, in spite of aching laziness of head and limbs.

CHAPTER THREE

I was ill after my visits to Wuthering Heights, but Mrs. Dean continued to entertain me with her story, and so the time passed.

She said Catherine behaved better at Thrushcross Grange than might have been expected. Edgar and his sister were careful not to ruffle her temper, and for a while all seemed well. But one evening as the housekeeper stood outside the kitchen door, a deep voice said, "Nelly, is that you?" And she knew the peaceful times were ended. Heathcliff had returned.

Catherine was breathless with excitement at the news. Her husband was much less pleased, as one might guess. He allowed Catherine to receive Heathcliff in the parlor, but his manner was cold.

Heathcliff had changed greatly. His manner was dignified, his face intelligent.

"I just heard of your marriage, Cathy," he said in a low tone. "I had planned to murder Hindley, but your warm welcome has changed my mind. Still, you'll not drive me off again. I've fought through a bitter life since I last heard your voice, and it was all for you."

During the days that followed, Catherine was wildly happy. Her friend visited Wuthering Heights and found himself a gambling partner in his old enemy Hindley Earnshaw. Soon Heathcliff was living there, within walking distance of the Grange. He came often. Edgar tried to hide his resentment, but when he learned that his sister Isabella was attracted to Heathcliff, he was much disturbed.

Catherine, too, tried to discourage her. "Heathcliff is no rough diamond," she warned. "He is a fierce, wolfish man who could never love a Linton. He might marry you for your fortune, but that is all."

Isabella believed not a word, though Mrs. Dean assured her that Catherine was Heathcliff's dearest friend and would not paint him worse than he was.

Things went badly at Wuthering Heights. Joseph told of all-night gambling, with Hindley losing constantly to his guest. Between games, Heathcliff came to the Grange, and one day Catherine teased Isabella in front of him.

"Isabella swears that the love Edgar has for me is nothing to that she entertains for you, Heathcliff," she said. Her sister-in-law ran sobbing from the room.

"You'd hear of odd things if I lived with that waxen face," Heathcliff said cruelly. "I'd turn those blue eyes black, every day or two. They are too much like your husband's." But he was interested in what she had said. Isabella would be her brother's heir if Catherine had no sons. The greed and hate in Heathcliff's soul made this important.

One day Mrs. Dean decided to visit the Heights. She found that Hareton no longer remembered her, and he swore horribly when she asked about his father. It was plain that Heathcliff was his hero and was directing all that happened in the house. She left, sick at heart.

Then came a terrible scene that changed all their lives. Catherine discovered that Heathcliff intended to make use of Isabella's love. He wanted to hurt her as he had been hurt when he learned Catherine had married. There was a frightening argument, with Catherine becoming ever more violent. Edgar heard them, and he ordered Heathcliff from the Grange. Edgar was clearly the weaker of the two men, both in body and spirit, but he acted bravely. Heathcliff was forced to leave when the gardener and his helpers were called.

Afterward Catherine dashed upstairs. "Tell Edgar if he provokes me again, I will become seriously ill," she cried.

"If I cannot keep Heathcliff for my friend, I'll break both their hearts by breaking my own!"

The next morning her door was locked. For two days she refused to see anyone or take food. Edgar waited in his study for her rage to pass.

On the third day she opened her door. Her appearance was ghastly! At first Mrs. Dean believed that she was acting out of spite and was not truly ill. But as Catherine raved on, it became clear she was delirious. "Nobody loves me," she said. "No one would ever miss me." Edgar looked at her with horrified astonishment. She seemed mad and vowed that soon she would be lying in the churchyard. Edgar could not control her.

As if this were not trouble enough, there were rumors that Isabella had been seen with Heathcliff on the moors. One morning she was not in her room. The milk-boy told of seeing her with Heathcliff, riding away toward Gimmerton.

Edgar was very bitter. "She went willingly," he said. "Now she is my sister in name only. She has disowned me." He told Mrs. Dean to send his sister's belongings to her new home, wherever it was.

CHAPTER FOUR

During the two months that followed, Heathcliff and Isabella remained absent. Edgar cared for Catherine devotedly. He tried to believe that when her body was healed, her mind would be restored also.

Her mood was dark. "I shall be on the moor only once more," she said, "and then I shall remain there forever." Edgar tried hard to cheer her, for on her life now depended another. In a little while an heir was to be born.

Isabella wrote a note to her brother from Wuthering Heights, asking for his forgiveness. It went unanswered. Then Mrs. Dean received a letter herself.

"I have two questions," it said. "First, how were you able to remain human when you lived here? And second, is Heathcliff a man or a devil? My life is a misery. Hindley Earnshaw is close to madness. He wishes only to win back his fortune from Heathcliff and then send him to hell. Joseph and Hareton treat me with the greatest contempt. As for Heathcliff, I do hate him and wish with all my heart I was back at the Grange. I am wretched, but you must tell no one. Just come to see me yourself."

Mrs. Dean told Edgar his sister longed to see him. When he declined to go, she decided to go herself. She found the house in a dreary state and Isabella pale and untidy.

Heathcliff greeted the housekeeper in quite friendly fashion. He began at once to ask for news of Catherine. The housekeeper answered plainly.

"She brought her illness on herself, but you can help her

now by not seeing her again. I can tell you that she is as different from your old friend as your wife is from me. In appearance and character she is greatly changed. You will only make her sick again, if you see her now, after she has nearly forgotten you."

"Forgotten me!" Heathcliff would not hear of it. "You must help me arrange a meeting. You shall not leave here until you agree." He spoke with the greatest passion of his love for Catherine and his hatred for the wife whom he had married only to spite Edgar.

When he threatened to force his way into the Grange if Mrs. Dean didn't help him, she agreed to take a letter to Catherine. Was she right or wrong? At the time she thought there was nothing else she could do.

That evening Mrs. Dean had a strong feeling that Heathcliff was waiting nearby. When Edgar went out, she put the letter in Catherine's hand. The invalid paid no attention to it until the housekeeper said, "It is from Heathcliff. He wishes to see you." Then she looked troubled and sighed.

Even as they spoke, a step sounded in the hall, and Heathcliff strode into the room.

He grasped Catherine in his arms. For five minutes he held her, kissing her and looking with agony into her face. Mrs. Dean knew what he saw — there was no chance of recovery. She was fated to die.

"Oh, Cathy! Oh, my life! How can I bear it?" he wept.

Catherine returned his look, but then her mood changed. She accused him and Edgar of having broken her heart. Bitterly she insisted he would forget her when she was dead.

"You will find others to love," she cried.

He turned away to hide his pain, and then her mood shifted again. She pleaded with him to come to her. In her eagerness she actually rose and sprang toward him. They met in an embrace which Mrs. Dean thought the invalid could not survive. She looked as if she had fainted. But

then her hand moved to clasp his neck. He broke into a torrent of reproaches, accusing her of betraying him and herself by her marriage.

"I have not broken your heart, *you* have broken it," he cried. "And what kind of life will it be for me when you — oh, God! Would *you* choose to live with your soul in the grave?"

They wept together while Mrs. Dean watched in dismay. Then she glanced out the window and saw Edgar coming up the road.

"Don't go!" Catherine shrieked. "It is the last time! Heathcliff, I shall die!"

She clung to him. Neither of them would listen to the housekeeper's warnings. Edgar hurried upstairs, alarmed by their voices, and when he saw his uninvited guest he went pale with rage. What he meant to do Mrs. Dean could not tell, for before Edgar could act, Heathcliff thrust Catherine's unconscious form into his arms.

"Help her first!" he ordered. "Then you shall speak to me." He left the room, telling the housekeeper that he would stay all night in the garden.

About twelve that night the baby Catherine was born. Her mother died soon afterward. Edgar's pain was almost unbearable.

When he rested at last, exhausted by his sorrow, Mrs. Dean slipped away to the garden. She found Heathcliff already sure of Catherine's death. He was bitter beyond imagining.

"Where is she now?" he cried. "I pray one prayer — that she not rest as long as I am living! Haunt me, Cathy — do not leave me alone. I cannot live without my life and my soul!"

He dashed his head against a tree trunk and howled more like a beast than a man. Mrs. Dean watched in horror, until he recovered enough to see her and order her away.

The Friday after Catherine's funeral, the Grange had a most unexpected visitor. Isabella burst into the house.

"I have run away at last," she said. "I shall never return to that devil. He has been more cruel than ever since Catherine's death. He nearly killed Hindley in a fit of rage. I would like to stay here and help you care for Catherine's baby, but he would never let me. I must go far enough that he cannot find me."

Mrs. Dean helped her pack some clothes, and she was driven away in the carriage, never to return. They heard that she bore a son a few months later and named him Linton.

One day Mrs. Dean met Heathcliff in the village, and he asked if she knew where Isabella was. She refused to tell him, but other servants did. He swore that some day, when he was ready, he would take the child from her.

Though Edgar grieved terribly for his lost wife, he was a good, brave man, and he did not indulge in anger and bitterness at his loss. He loved his child deeply, because she was Catherine's daughter. He trusted God. How different he was from Hindley Earnshaw who became a lost soul when his wife died!

Mrs. Dean found it strange that she thought so much about Hindley just then, for only a few days later she learned he had joined his sister Catherine in death. Mrs. Dean grieved for him, because she remembered the days when they had been children together. She persuaded Edgar to ask for Hareton to come to the Grange to live.

"Tell your master I have a fancy to try my hand at rearing a young one," Heathcliff told Mrs. Dean. "If he takes Hareton, I will claim my own child from Isabella and raise him here."

Edgar said nothing more. Heathcliff now owned Wuthering Heights; Hindley had lost it all through gambling. Hareton, who should have been the first gentleman of the neighborhood, would live as a servant, unable to help himself and too ignorant even to know he was wronged.

CHAPTER FIVE

I still required rest, so Mrs. Dean had many quiet hours in which to continue her story. She described the next twelve years as happy ones. Little Cathy grew into a lively beauty. Her father never spoke a harsh word to her. He kept her at home and taught her himself.

Sometimes she looked over the moors to the crags in the distance and longed to go there. But Edgar would never allow it. The road passed too close to Wuthering Heights.

One day Edgar received a letter from Isabella. She was very ill and wanted to see him to talk about her son. Edgar was gone three weeks, leaving Cathy at home. She spent the summer days riding around Thrushcross Park, and one evening she did not return. A worker said he had seen her riding toward the crags.

Mrs. Dean hurried off in search of her. When she reached Wuthering Heights, she saw one of Cathy's dogs lying outside the door. The housekeeper admitted her, and there was Cathy talking to Hareton Earnshaw. He was a big, rough-looking lad now.

Mrs. Dean scolded Cathy fiercely. "If you knew whose house this was, you'd be glad to leave it," she said.

"It's your father's, isn't it?" Cathy asked Hareton. He shook his head.

"Your master's then?"

Hareton swore and turned away.

"This is your cousin, Miss Cathy," said the housekeeper. "He is not a servant."

"My cousin!" Cathy laughed scornfully. "He is not!"

Mrs. Dean was angry with them all and wanted only to leave before Heathcliff should appear. When they set out for home, Cathy talked about her day. Hareton's dogs had attacked hers, and to soothe her he had guided her to the crags. She had liked him until the housekeeper had called him her cousin.

Mrs. Dean told her in return that her father disliked everyone at Wuthering Heights. If he found out Cathy had visited there, he would be angry with both of them. He might even send Mrs. Dean away.

Cathy promised she would never tell.

A letter arrived to say Isabella had died. Soon afterward Edgar returned from his trip to see her, bringing young Linton with him. He was a sickly child. Cathy was eager for a playmate, but she was forced to treat him like a baby instead. She kissed his cheek and offered him tea in her saucer.

No sooner were the children in bed than Joseph arrived at the door. He had come to claim Heathcliff's son!

"You shall not tonight!" Edgar told him, and he ordered the fierce old man to leave. But he knew Linton could not be kept at the Grange if Heathcliff wanted him. Early the next morning the boy and Mrs. Dean set out for Wuthering Heights together.

Linton was puzzled. He hadn't known he had a father!

"How strange that he never came to see Mamma and me!" he said.

Heathcliff met them at his door. "You've brought my property," he said. "Let me see it." Then he laughed scornfully. "What a chicken he is!"

"Be kind to the boy," Mrs. Dean begged.

"Oh, I will be," Heathcliff said. "He is sickly looking, but I want him to live long enough to inherit your master's estate. He shall have a fine room and a tutor, even though I despise him."

31

There was little more to be said. Mrs. Dean slipped away as soon as possible, with Linton's cries ringing in her ears:

"Don't leave me! I'll not stay here!"

She could only hope that Heathcliff would remember how frail the child was and treat him accordingly.

Cathy was never told where Linton Heathcliff had gone. Mrs. Dean heard later, from Heathcliff's housekeeper, that the boy was very unhappy. He was selfish, disagreeable, and often ill. Heathcliff could hardly bear to be near him. Hareton talked to him once in a while, but the visits usually ended in angry words.

Time wore on at the Grange in its pleasant way. On Cathy's sixteenth birthday, she and Mrs. Dean went for a walk on the edge of the moor. They were to be gone only an hour, but as they left the gate Cathy ran on ahead. When Mrs. Dean caught up, she was dismayed to see Cathy in conversation with Heathcliff and Hareton.

"Is that your son?" she was asking, pointing at Hareton. "I have seen him before."

Heathcliff said it was not, but he had a son at home — someone Cathy had already met. He invited her to Wuthering Heights, and Cathy, full of curiosity, insisted on going.

"Your father will be very angry," Mrs. Dean said. But Heathcliff pulled the housekeeper along. "I want her to see Linton," he said softly. "My plan is that the two cousins fall in love and get married. I wish this and intend to have it."

There was no end to the man's hatred for Edgar Linton. He wished to steal the girl away and make her share the misery of life at Wuthering Heights. Mrs. Dean watched in despair as Cathy greeted Linton joyfully and promised to visit him often.

"But you mustn't tell your father," Heathcliff said. "He and I have quarrelled, and he would not want you to come."

Hareton had left the room, but he returned now with his face washed and his hair combed. Cathy remembered now what the housekeeper had said on her first visit to Wuthering Heights. She demanded to know if Hareton was really her cousin, and she jeered at him cruelly when assured that he was.

"I have made Hareton into what I was at his age," Heathcliff said in a low voice to Mrs. Dean. "He suffers as I did, because I have kept him ignorant and coarse. Oh, how his father would grieve if he could see him now!"

When they returned home to the Grange, Cathy could not hold her tongue about the visit.

"Heathcliff is a wicked man," her father scolded her. He told her how her Aunt Isabella had been treated and how Heathcliff had won Wuthering Heights from Hindley Earnshaw. After much arguing, she sadly agreed not to go there again.

But Mrs. Dean kept close watch. She soon discovered that letters full of affection were being sent to Linton, and answers received.

"I'll tell your father unless you promise to stop writing," Mrs. Dean threatened. Cathy sobbed bitterly, but she finally agreed.

In the autumn of the year Edgar Linton caught a bad cold. Cathy worried greatly about him. One day as she walked with Mrs. Dean, Heathcliff suddenly appeared before them. He spoke harshly to Cathy. Young Linton Heathcliff was also sick.

"You broke Linton's heart when you stopped writing," he said. "I doubt that he will live through the winter. He dreams of you night and day."

All the way home and all that evening Cathy wept over his words. "I shall never feel at ease till I see Linton," she sobbed. "I must tell him it isn't my fault that I do not write."

The next day Mrs. Dean could not bear her young mistress's sorrow any longer. She gave in, and the two of them set out for Wuthering Heights.

CHAPTER SIX

It was a cold, misty morning, Mrs. Dean recalled. She and Cathy found Linton lying in the parlor at Wuthering Heights. He was sick and bad-tempered.

"Why didn't you come before?" he demanded. "You should have come instead of writing. Those long letters tired me. Fix the fire at once!"

"Are you glad I've come?" Cathy asked.

"Yes," he replied. "Papa said you despised me, but you don't, do you?"

Cathy assured him that, next to her father and Mrs. Dean, she loved him best. But talk of love did not bring peace, for they soon fell to arguing over whether husbands and wives must love each other.

"Your mother hated your father," said Linton. "And she loved mine."

In a rage, Cathy pushed his chair, causing him to fall against one arm. He began to cough, continuing so long that his visitors were frightened. At last he was soothed, but only after Cathy promised to come again to repair the damage she had done.

On the way home, Mrs. Dean scolded her for her promise.

"Linton is the worst-tempered slip that ever struggled into its teens," she said. "Small loss to his family when he drops off!"

But Cathy defended him. "I can help him get better," she insisted. "We won't quarrel when we are used to each other."

The long wet walk took its toll. For the next three weeks Mrs. Dean was sick. Cathy spent her days nursing her father and the housekeeper, with only the nights for herself. At the end of that time, Mrs. Dean discovered that her young mistress had ridden each evening to Wuthering Heights.

"Promise not to be angry," Cathy begged. "I'll tell you all that happened."

Some of the visits were pleasant, she said, but most were full of quarrels and complaining. Heathcliff stayed out of sight, and Hareton was seldom seen. Once he told Cathy that he had learned to read his name, but she had laughed at him and he had skulked away.

"He is your cousin, you know," Mrs. Dean scolded. "He was as bright a child as you were. It is only Heathcliff that has made him as he is."

But Cathy insisted that Hareton was a brute. That same evening, as she and Linton talked by the fire, Hareton had burst in and ordered them from the room.

"You shall not keep me out!" he roared.

Linton had become sick with rage and was carried off to bed. Cathy had ridden away, sobbing. When Hareton followed her to say he was sorry, she had cut him with her whip and ordered him off.

At her next visit, to her surprise, Linton blamed her for the scene of the night before.

"If I make you ill, I will not come again," she told him.

But then he spoke so sadly, she had to forgive him.

"I know I am cross and bitter," he said. "Papa says I am worthless, and he is right. Your kindness has made me love you, Cathy. I cannot help my nature, but I am sorry for it."

So the visits continued. When Mrs. Dean had heard the whole story, she went with it to Edgar Linton. The result was that Edgar wrote a letter to his nephew Linton. He told the boy he could visit the Grange when he pleased, but Cathy would not come again to Wuthering Heights.

Time passed and Edgar grew more ill. He feared for Cathy's future. If Linton could make her happy, he would be pleased to have them marry, even though the boy was Heathcliff's son. He wrote to his nephew again, and the replies seemed to please him. Heathcliff must have watched Linton's letters carefully, taking out all complaints and talk of illness. When Linton begged for a meeting with Cathy on the moors, Edgar agreed, as long as Mrs. Dean went along.

They found the boy lying on the heath alone. He was clearly very sick and cared little about seeing them. He was there because his father had sent him.

"Promise you'll return next Thursday," he begged. "You must! And don't tell my father I acted sickly or dull."

Cathy promised. The next week Linton was even worse. When Cathy suggested he would be better off at home, he broke into tears.

"Don't go," he sobbed. "Leave me, and I shall be killed."

As they talked, Heathcliff appeared. He asked the visitors to return to Wuthering Heights for tea.

"You must come," Linton begged. "I'm not to return to the house without you."

Heathcliff told him to be still, but Linton clung to his cousin until she agreed to go.

When they reached the house, Heathcliff closed the door behind them and locked it. Suddenly frightened, Cathy tried to get the key from him. He slapped her viciously, then left them alone in the parlor.

"Papa wishes us to be married," Linton explained. "He's afraid I shall die before your father, if we wait. Then I won't inherit your father's land. You must stay tonight and marry me tomorrow."

Cathy sobbed wildly. She was sure her father would die of worry. When Heathcliff returned, she said she would gladly marry Linton, if only she could return to her father at once to tell him she was all right.

Heathcliff would not listen. For the next four days, Mrs. Dean was locked in an upstairs room. She saw no one but Hareton, who brought her food. On the fifth morning the housekeeper, Zillah, appeared. She had just returned from a journey. She had been told Mrs. Dean and Cathy were at the Heights because they had been lost on the moors and rescued by Heathcliff.

Mrs. Dean hurried downstairs. She found Linton by the fire eating candy.

"Cathy is locked in her room because she will not stop crying," he complained. "She is my wife now, but she keeps crying, though I order her to stop."

Mrs. Dean begged him to free the girl, but he would not do it. At last she left, determined to bring help from the Grange.

Edgar was close to death when she reached home. For a while he revived at the news that his child was safe. Mrs. Dean explained that they had been held against their wills at the Heights.

Later that night there was a rap at the door, and Cathy burst into the house. She had at last persuaded Linton to free her. She rushed to her father's bedside and was with him the rest of the night, until, near dawn, he died.

The next day a lawyer appointed by Heathcliff arrived. He sent away all the servants, except Mrs. Dean. The funeral was to be hurried, he said, and Cathy — now Mrs. Linton Heathcliff — was allowed to stay at the Grange only until her father's corpse had left it.

CHAPTER SEVEN

The evening after the funeral, Heathcliff came to carry the young mistress off to Wuthering Heights. Mrs. Dean was to stay at the Grange. While Cathy gathered her things, Heathcliff talked to the housekeeper.

"Do you know what I did yesterday?" he demanded fiercely. "I had Catherine's grave opened so I could look once more on her face. For all the eighteen years since she left me I have begged her spirit to haunt me, but she has remained out of reach. Always I look for her and almost find her. Still, she has not shown herself to me. Now that I've seen her face again, I am calmed — a little. And I have bribed the sexton to remove one side of her coffin. When I die, he will do the same thing to my coffin, and she and I will lie together."

The farewell that followed this fearful talk was painful for Mrs. Dean and Cathy. The housekeeper was told to stay away from Wuthering Heights. In the months that followed, her only news came from Zillah, the housekeeper, who did not like the girl.

Zillah said that Linton had been close to death when Cathy returned. Heathcliff would not have a doctor, and Cathy was left to do the nursing. It was harsh work, for Linton demanded care every hour of the day. When at last he died, Cathy refused to speak to any of the household.

"When I would have given my life for one kind word, you all kept off," she said, not caring that it was Heathcliff who had ordered it so.

"And that is how things stand now," Mrs. Dean said, reaching the end of her sad story. She said she had thought of taking a cottage for herself and Cathy, but she knew Heathcliff would not allow it. The girl must live, in misery, at Wuthering Heights.

By this time my illness had passed, and I decided to leave the lonely moors. I rode one day to the Heights to tell Heathcliff I would not stay for the balance of my lease. He was not home, but Cathy and Hareton were there. It was as Zillah had reported to Mrs. Dean; they could not speak civilly to each other. Cathy jeered at her cousin's continuing attempts to read, and he responded with rage. The argument I witnessed ended with Hareton throwing his books into the fire.

It was a relief when Heathcliff returned. I quickly settled my business with him and left. Soon after that I left Yorkshire.

1802

This September I traveled north to hunt and found myself near the Grange. A new housekeeper was there. She said Mrs. Dean had moved to Wuthering Heights.

I decided to go there. The walk across the moors was beautiful, and when I arrived at the gate, I found it unlocked for the first time.

This is an improvement, I thought. And as I reached the house, I was surprised to hear happy voices from within. A peek at a window showed a handsome young man and a lovely girl engaged in a reading lesson.

"Read it again," Cathy said. "For the third time, you dunce!"

And Hareton did so, ending with a request for a kiss as his reward.

As I watched, they stood and went to a door, evidently planning a walk on the moors. I hurried around a corner and found Mrs. Dean there, singing to herself.

She was delighted to see me. She brought me ale, and for the next hour she told me of the most recent events at Wuthering Heights.

Heathcliff was dead!

"Three months since," she said. "Soon after you left, he called me to take Zillah's place as housekeeper. I found Cathy changed, quite irritable and restless. She wasn't allowed to leave the garden, and she spent much time teasing Hareton and trying to make him talk to her."

Mrs. Dean soon realized that Cathy was sorry she had taunted her cousin. Finally the girl went so far as to tell him so. He was a stubborn young man, but at last he yielded to her smiles. They began to read together and became friends instead of enemies.

When Heathcliff noticed the change, he was furious. For a moment it seemed that he would surely punish the girl, but then he gazed into her face and hesitated. It must have been a vision of his Catherine he saw there. After that, the sight of Cathy and Hareton, who looked even more like Catherine, disturbed him deeply. He avoided them whenever possible.

He told Mrs. Dean that a change had come into his life. He could not say what it was, but the real world meant nothing to him. One night he stayed away till dawn, and when he returned his eyes held a strange, joyful glitter. He would not eat, nor did he take food for several days after that. He talked to no one but seemed always to be looking at a space just a few feet away. He smiled a ghastly smile. He did not sleep.

"Are we alone?" he said to Mrs. Dean one day. When she assured him they were, he went on staring at a spot about two yards away. Whatever he saw, it gave him the greatest pleasure and pain as he followed it with his eyes.

He cared for nothing. "Don't tell me I must eat and rest," he said. "You might as well bid a man struggling in the water to rest within an arm's length of shore! I must reach it first, and then I'll rest."

On the morning of the fifth day of this strange time, Mrs. Dean noticed that Heathcliff's window was swinging open in the rain. She hurried upstairs and found him lying dead. His eyes met hers in a fierce look. He seemed to smile. When she tried to close the eyes, she could not, and his parted lips sneered at her for trying.

Hareton, the most wronged, was the only one who mourned. He wept all night and kissed that savage face that others could hardly bear to look at. He had a generous heart and was chained to Heathcliff by habit.

The master was buried exactly as he had requested, much to the scandal of the neighborhood. Mrs. Dean said the country folk believe he walks the moor with Catherine even now.

"I don't believe it," the housekeeper told me, "but I shall be glad when we leave this grim place. Cathy and Hareton will marry soon, and we shall move to Thrushcross Grange. Joseph will stay to take care of this house."

As I left that evening, I saw the young lovers return from their walk. They are afraid of nothing, I thought. Later I stopped at the churchyard and visited the three graves on a slope next to the moor. Edgar, Catherine, Heathcliff. The soft wind blew through the grass, and I wondered how anyone could imagine unquiet slumbers for the sleepers in that quiet earth.

A WUTHERING HEIGHTS FAMILY TREE

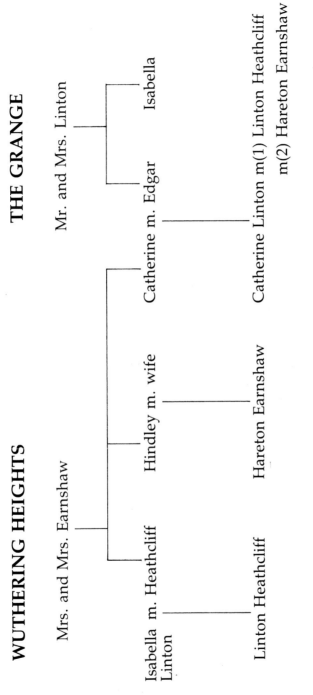

GLOSSARY

console (kən sol´)   to give comfort and take away the sense of grief

contempt (kən tempt´)   a feeling of hatred and lack of respect

delirious (di lir´ ē əs)   being confused and disturbed

disown (dis ōn´)   to cut off any connection with someone

haughty (hot´ ē)   being very proud and scornful

invalid (in´ və ləd)   a person who is sick or disabled

moor (moor)   an area of open, rolling land

sexton (sek´ stən)   a worker at a church who takes care of church property